c
o
p
e

GREEN LIGHTS

(Kyle Muntz)

—The Spectrum—

Green

Blue

Red

Green

Dark Green

Blue

Black

Green

GREEN

I want to talk about color.

::::::::::::::::::::::

A line of trees spread back along the streets. And then there was the neighborhood. The neighborhood was endless, and older than anyone could remember. All the houses were very neat and very clean, even if not many people lived in them. The leaves never fell and the grass never grew.

::::::::::::::::::::::

I want to talk about color.

::::::::::::::::::::::

There was a girl in the tree above me. She jumped out of it. When she landed, she didn't make a sound.

It was E. She seemed to be having a nice day.

"I knew you were there," she said. "I saw you."

"You have a leaf in your hair," I said.

It was nice.

"Here," she said, "you can have it."

I held it against the sun until the edge of the leaf caught fire, and I had to give it to the wind.

"Look, it's burning."

"It's pretty," she said. "The color isn't the same."

"It's changing."

From green to red to something else.

And then there was no more leaf.

::::::::::::::::::::::

We had a conversation about poison apples destroying faces. The apples grow on trees, except they're invisible. This is a strange world, full of strange things.

Evil spreads out of them. Evil spreads out of a lot of things.

::::::::::::::::::::::

There was a mountain in the distance.

::::::::::::::::::::::

We spent a while looking around. It was that kind of day.

"Before I go," I asked, "could you give me a kiss?"

She did, and that was really nice too.

I want to talk about color.

::::::::::::::::::::::

An old man lives on my street, past a couple of houses but still on my street. His face is shaped like a skull, and not just because there's a skull behind it. Every day, he wears a suit, and carries a cane with a serpent on top, bearing its teeth and writhing. In the morning he stands outside his house or on a corner, narrowing his eyes. His wrinkled hands are like claws, with sharp nails at their ends. The snake bites children when they pass, and sometimes, if it knocks them down for long enough, the old man eats them.

This old man is pure evil. His soul is like a pitcher with all the water poured of it. His stare is impossibly frightening, but fortunately, he's far too old to be in horror movies. No light shines from his body. If you were to look inside, no matter how hard you tried, you would find no light anywhere.

Sometimes, when it's safe, I talk to him. The most

important thing is to keep your distance and be ready when he lunges. I've gotten talented at dodging him; if this were a martial arts movie I would say I moved like water, but the truth was that I moved like nothing, meaning I wasn't there. I wasn't anywhere. Usually he gives up after a few minutes and forgets to try for a while after that.

"The ends of his teeth are sharp. They gnash when he talks."

"I'm curious," I said. "Where did you get your cane?"

"I captured a man and forced him to make it for me. He fused the spirit of a serpent to the most dangerous weapon in all the world. And then he gave it to me."

"What happened to him after that?"

"Do you really have to ask?"

...Did I?

::::::::::::::::::::::

For the first time in this life, I really will talk about color. Color fell on the leaves and turned them visible. Color fell onto the grass where it grew. Color twisted a veil in the sky. Color surrounded and filled this visual world. Color, in itself, became everything (omnipresent, ever-present, the only present). Color revealed and fabricated the world.

But no.

This wasn't what I meant to talk about.

::::::::::::::::::::::

I want to forget about seeing.

::::::::::::::::::::::

E and I spent the morning sitting outside.

We were trying to drink water, but the light kept making it evaporate. That's the problem with setting things in the sun. They melt, and disappear out of the universe.

Not far away, with just his head showing over the fence, I saw the old man. He was whittling a stick with his teeth; bits of squirrel were stuck between them. He had a hunter's eyes, emphasizing his pointed chin, sickly grinning. He liked to eat things and laugh about it. Making them disappear.

"Hey," I pointed at him, "look over there, do you see him?"

She saw.

"Be really careful."

"Why?"

"He's scary, and he likes to hurt people."

15

She nodded, and said the old man was kind of ugly, too.

We looked at him and made faces. When he didn't go away we started to throw things: rotten fruit, rubber, paper cups, a chair. One hit him and he growled; he picked up a rock and started chewing on it. Bits of stone crumbled until finally he crushed it through the center.

After that, we were especially careful. Like I said, he was scary.

::::::::::::::::::::::

I went walking with E in the forest. We went to the river and threw rocks at the waterfall. Then we put our heads beneath the water and tried to breathe, and it was nice, even if it didn't work.

Yeah, it was nice.

::::::::::::::::::::::

I found the old man in his usual place; as expected, he had not gotten any younger. His teeth kept grinding together, chewing something that made his face look funny. Every few seconds he would shift it against his cheek. His back was even crookeder than normal, almost enough that his spine stuck out. Bird shit clung to his shoulder. It was hard not to notice.

"Gross," I said.

"What?"

"Nothing," I replied, "it's nothing."

"I don't like you, you know that?"

"I figured."

"The way you stand annoys me. When you talk, it makes me angry." He coughed. "And you move far too quickly."

"I'm sorry."

"And you're too willing to apologize," he said. "I hate people who apologize for the things they do."

The house across from us was very quiet. No one ever came to this part of the neighborhood, except me.

"You know," I said, "I'm not sure if I really like your ideas."

"That's the point," he said. "You aren't supposed to."

::::::::::::::::::::::

E was hiding in the bushes. She jumped out and pressed me into the ground.

I almost hit my head on a rock. It was pretty awkward.

"Are you comfortable?" she asked.

"Not really... no."

"Yesterday I saw a candle. It made me think of you."

"I'm touched."

"It was burning," she said, and told me how I was like a candle. Her eyes started to glass over, like xylophones.

Her hair fell from above so that it touched my face. It was like a kiss except it tickled more.

"Oh yeah," I said. "What were you doing in the bushes?"

"I was waiting for you."

"How did you know I would come this way?"

"It wasn't very difficult." She paused. "Don't you always come this way?"

"Yeah," I said.

I guess I do.

::::::::::::::::::::::

"I like your suit," I said. "It suits you."

"I like it too," the old man replied. "Particularly the stripes."

"Where did you get it?"

"A long time ago, I used to sell things on the radio. That's where I learned to use my voice." He cleared his throat, and spat out a piece of somebody's dog. "Every day when I came into work I would wear this suit, or one like it. I have a closet full of them."

Awkwardly, as if it hurt to move, he scratched his crotch. I shuddered. It was frightening to see.

"What did you sell?" I asked.

"Useless things," he replied. "The more useless the better."

"Fond memories?"

"I've never had a good memory," he said. "When I think about the past, all it does is make me hate the present more."

Fluttering its wings, a crow landed on his shoulder, and began to caw. Dark ink shot from its beak, a hideous vomit, so strong it made a hissing sound splattering against the sidewalk. The spray was powerful enough the crow nearly knocked itself down. A black pool formed, seeping outwards across the pavement. No fish swam in it. No fish could live in such a place.

"I really hate catfish," I said.

"For a long time," the old man replied, "I was the head of a company. The radio company. I took it over utilizing deceit, poison, sharp daggers, and pills to help with my indigestion." He chuckled, and picked a piece of fur from between his teeth. "I had stomach problems because of drinking so much blood."

"What happened?"

"To what?"

"Your money."

"Isn't it obvious?" he asked.

Television.

::::::::::::::::::::::

Nearby, behind an abandoned house, we found an immense flower growing from the ground. The flower was at least a hundred feet tall. Beads of water clung to its sides.

"Look," I said. "It's a flower."

"Who do you think planted it?" E asked.

"I don't know. But it really holds the view together. This part of the neighborhood."

She nodded. "It looks like a picture of itself, meaning it looks better than real. That means something. It implies amazingness."

"Should we climb it?"

"Probably," she said. "If we didn't, we would feel bad about it later."

We were holding hands and it was pretty cute.

"I kind of wish we could see the top," I said. "That would make this so much easier."

::::::::::::::::::::::

A quick movement. The old man lunged, and I barely stumbled out of the way.

His cane hit the ground a few feet to one side. The snake bit the cement, bruising its fangs. It quivered. It spat venom. Its eyes were black diamonds: corrupted.

"That was close," I said.

"Almost got you."

"Yeah," I replied. "You did."

"Just wait," he snickered. "You'll be mine." He began to pet the snake's head. It purred, curling around his wrist. Slithering.

::::::::::::::::::::::

On top of the flower, in its petals, we found a lake. The water was sweet because it was also nectar. We swam in it for a while. We could see our reflections on the bottom, illuminated in blue light.

It felt like floating. Into warmth, into the midst of a fountain.

Impossibly near, in all directions, we were surrounded by the sky. In truth it had always been that way; but there, at the cusp of it, daydreaming of seagulls, it just felt different, somehow.

I want to talk about color.

::::::::::::::::::::

I need somewhere to talk about my problems.
    First, I suppose, I should find some.

::::::::::::::::::::

M was telling me about his problems.
    "My body doesn't work anymore."
    "Any idea why?" I asked.
    "I accidentally crushed one of my ankles," he said. "An anvil fell on my head. One of my arms is missing." He shook his head. "And that fucking snake won't quit biting me. So now, instead of blood, I have venom."
    "You... need to see a doctor."
    "That's what I thought," he said, "but I can't find one. There's no help for us. No help anywhere in the world."
    That life is bitter as salt, with the taste of cracked ice.
    Remember then.

::::::::::::::::::::::

I sat outside, looking at the mountain in the distance. A bird flew around it. Or at least, I thought it was a bird.

::::::::::::::::::::::

That night there was a celebration in the neighborhood. We became pagan, drinking water. As the moon fell, we began to sing. Our voices echoed against the ceiling, reverberated against the windows. All of us were wearing masks. Mine was white with narrow eyes and bits of red paint on the front. The music of us glowed like something better than sound. It was breaking through boundaries. That is the greatest thing, to be in each of us. To be timeless; to be discovered.

M danced where he'd fallen. Tears fell across his eyes. He lifted himself off the ground. He poured the water across his face; it sparkled like dust. We were surrounded by trees. He looked up, still singing. At our backs, a waterfall fell upwards, into darkness.

"If you do this right," he said, "it reflects the moon."

BLUE

A blue light is shining on the neighborhood. I wonder where it comes from.

:::::::::::::::::::::

There's a girl who lives on my street. She spends her days playing violin and drinking water. Sometimes I think the whole purpose of life is just to spend time drinking water.

At night, she sleeps. In the morning, she wakes. Her downcast eyes observe without seeing. Her room is quiet; only she breathes in it. She sits. She plays music. The light is blue.

:::::::::::::::::::::

Blue light crawls over the street when I look out my window. Blue light hangs heavy in the curtains. The sidewalk is made of steps and stones that people walk on, with routine benches in it, beside buildings. People sit in the benches, and look out windows. Sometimes I watch them. That must be obvious, or I wouldn't know they were there.

That blue light is muffled as the curtains close, when the shadows stretch. My room contains a table, a bed, a window, and me. The world is only one color. Every morning, I look into the sky, hoping to see the sun rise. But no, there is only the moon.

::::::::::::::::::::::

Mr. B is a pilgrim. He spends all day reading books, listening to old jazz, eating pistachios. Wherever he goes, he is listening to music.

Look at this, he said, holding out a book. *Look closely.*
What is it?
It has words in it.
Imagine that.
Do you know what they do?
I never.
When you look at them, they make things.
Like what?
Not pictures.
I scoffed.

::::::::::::::::::::::

Am I here? Am I in the neighborhood?
The moon shone through the window and became

a girl. Her face in shadow, her figure negated.

Yeah, I said. *You're here.*

It's strange, she said. *Everything is so blue.*

::::::::::::::::::::::

Mr. B lives in a big house in an abandoned part of the neighborhood. The house is very old, and there are lots of bookshelves. Against one wall hangs a picture of a pyramid; and another of an old man with sharp teeth, whistling to himself, eating a gigantic piece of watermelon.

The blue light brings out the ghosts, Mr. B told me.

Any idea why?

I looked around. My neck hurt.

It's cold, he said. *They don't like the neighborhood with heat.* That day, in the street, I thought I saw a skull in the mist. It scowled, spat flame, and began to wail. Like everything else, its surface shone a dull blue.

All its teeth had been sharpened to points.

::::::::::::::::::::::

The moon said she liked being a girl. She was beautiful in the sense that light is beautiful.

I have a reason to be this way, she said. *I'm so tired of floating.*

I believe you.

Time passed.

I always wondered if the moon could become a person, I said.

Nothing changes, she said. *Everything exists, but nothing changes.*

To philosophize is to be defeated, more surely than a thing begins. We rolled in a glass orb defeated.

Our only thought occurred once, forever ago, to be endlessly remembered.

::::::::::::::::::::::

I saw Mr. B outside a restaurant selling top hats and coffee. He sat in his chair, reading a newspaper.

Hello, I said.

Look over there. He pointed. *Do you see her?*

What?

That woman has an umbrella. She's hitting someone with it.

Wow.

Yeah, I know, there's blood.

It'll be all right though—her arm should get tired soon. Probably.

This is a sick world, he said.

I agree.

We're sick, he said, *but there's no one to take our temperature. We're freezing. The ice is coming soon.*

He was right. I needed a sweater.

:::::::::::::::::::::::

The world froze.

Every morning, when I got up, I would open the window to knock the icicles away; then I would make breakfast, and drink coffee. Ice had taken over the world. Brushing my teeth was nearly impossible.

All day, wearing clothes, I huddled beneath blankets. My breath froze: first a mist, then a mass of droplets that fell like miniature hail.

I had forgotten to pay the heating bill.

:::::::::::::::::::::::

On the streets, I saw a big group of people, all wearing thick coats with fur lining their faces, pulling treasure chests attached to heavy chains. They were everywhere—sidewalks, rooftops, the middle of the road—all moving slowly, almost like zombies; but I could see the breath as it encircled their bodies, misting just barely, so I knew they were alive: each with their head down, back bent, shoulders forward, dragging a treasure chest. It was impossible to know where they were going. Even if I were to ask, I doubted I would receive an answer.

31

:::::::::::::::::::::

After much effort, I thawed my room.

I'm not proud of the things I did to accomplish this.

(I got a job carrying a flamethrower around the neighborhood, melting people. My coworkers treated me like shit.)

:::::::::::::::::::::

Like a kid, I slid down a hill, pretending my body was a sled. At the base, breathing hard, I decided I really wanted a cup of coffee. When I stood to get it, somebody came up and tackled me. And didn't get off. If I hadn't pushed him, I might have been buried in the snow.

What was that about?

I'm not going to describe quite what happened, but by the time I got him to stop, the other guy had a branch stuck in his stomach. He must have been afraid to take it out. He just looked at it, and wiggled the end a bit.

I hate you, he replied.

For what?

From some direction that wasn't ours, wind blew.

A mandala of leaves let fall copious teardrops of blue snow

The bottom of the hill was a thought and a place and a color. It had two people and a bunch of trees in it.

You should probably get that looked at. I pointed at his stomach. *Sorry, I guess. Even though it's your fault.*

This is nothing, he groaned. *Just a flesh wound.*

Still, you're bleeding.

Someday, he said, *I'll get you.*

I scratched my chin. *You sound like somebody else. An old man.*

What?

It's nothing, don't worry about it. I waved my hand. *Get out of here. You might get eaten by a bear. The ghosts have come out.*

That's ridiculous. There aren't any bears around here.

I'm not so sure. Behind him, I saw the flaming skeleton of an animal, hideously thin, extending its claws; and above that, yes—its eyes glowing green, drool frozen around its mouth—the head of a bear. No mammoth sounds of it; there are fields in this country. Each field we pass smells of sewage and cranberries.

::::::::::::::::::::::

I was walking through the inside of a school and met

Mr. B there too. I could tell it was him because I could hear really loud jazz from down the hall, miles outside the building. Today he'd brought a table with him. He was reading a manual about how to dissect octopuses, and Proust.

There are already enough Frenchmen in the world, he said. *In France.*

Somebody walked outside the room, holding their ears, which had begun to bleed. I wondered if they would be deaf later. Mr. B told me that I should be afraid of octopuses.

You were right, I said, *about the weather.*

What do you expect? He laughed. *The sky can only go so long without a moon.*

::::::::::::::::::::::

The moon took a bath, whirled in steam. Because of the bathtub, I couldn't help noticing that her skin was the color of porcelain—and for the first time in the history of words, it was finally true.

Outside, the ice pressed against walls that were about to collapse.

She lowered her eyes. *What are you thinking about?*

Snow shovels. When they have snow in them, they're really hard to lift.

Am I doing the wrong thing? I like these people. I like this

34

neighborhood.

No.

You're lying, I can tell. It's so cold.

I told her everything was fine, but I don't think she believed me.

::::::::::::::::::::::

The moon returned to the sky and it was all my fault.

RED

Look at those banisters.

:::::::::::::::::::::

I woke up in a classroom, with other people. Because the door was glass, I could see out into the hallway.

We were all in the back of the room, rolling around on a big bed. A girl sat on top of me. Another put her hand into my face.

—You're in my spot, the girl on top of me said.

The door opened.

A woman entered.

:::::::::::::::::::::

The woman called me to the front of the room and hit me in the face with a stapler. A few minutes later the blood went away.

—What do you do on your days off? I asked.

—I graze horses, cook lunch, and watch television.

—That sounds fun.

I've always kind of wanted to fall off a horse.

::::::::::::::::::::::::

She asked me a question.

I never know the answers to questions.

::::::::::::::::::::::::

We rolled around on the bed for a little bit longer. We threw the paper cranes around until someone got hit in the eye, and it started to bleed, and they ran around for a while with a paper crane sticking out of their face.

It's all meaningless. It's all happening.

—You should go, someone told me.

Ten years hating acupuncture.

—Why?

—There's no place for you here.

I felt rejected. I felt lost in universe of all one color.

::::::::::::::::::::::::

Outside the room everything was red. A red hallway, a red carpet, red ceiling. The building looked sort of like a school crossed with an abandoned castle, full of corridors and balconies, and huge open chambers.

I stopped when I met a girl inspecting a statue. It had a detachable penis, and she kept doing all kinds of strange things to it. Her clothes were still on, but that didn't make it less strange. It made it stranger. The statue had no idea. It stared in some other direction, never at her, fascinated by nothing, stuck in some ridiculous pose, pelvis thrust forward (minus the phallus, of course).

—What are you doing? I asked.

—Playing it like a flute, she said. See?

—I do, but why?

—I don't need a reason. If I did, I wouldn't be doing this.

Suddenly, I felt shame in my face. She narrowed her eyes. Other people passed without stopping. I was invading her privacy. I was an invader.

—Do you understand?

The marble penis, still clutched between her fingers, was unnecessarily long, thick, and laced with veins, so big it could even have been used as a weapon. I was a little confused, I think, about why someone would make a statue like that.

I walked until the wall beside me became a pane of glass. Behind it was a laboratory, full of long rectangular tables. People walked between them, wearing red coats and red goggles.

I stopped, and somebody came out through a clear space I hadn't realized was a door. Her face sparkled. It was kind of annoying.

—There you are, she said.

I nodded.

I was there.

—We've been waiting for you. Stay here. I'll be back soon.

A minute later she returned carrying something in both hands. It was ugly, and wiggly.

She handed me an octopus.

It latched onto my face; it latched around my arms; there were tentacles everywhere; it was gross, and had a funny smell; and when it moved it made a low, wet sound, like someone dragging their foot along the beach when the sand was damp; and its eye faced the other direction, but I couldn't see, because there was an octopus in the way.

—Its name is Gregory, she said. Make sure to be polite.

I tried to give it back to her, but all I did was walk into the wall.

::::::::::::::::::::::

I took a deep breath, feeling sorry for myself.

—Hello, said the octopus. My name is Gregory.

—So I've heard.

—I enjoy small fish and long walks on the beach.

—Could you be quiet for a minute? I'm not feeling

very good.

—I'm also a painter, the octopus continued. My work has been lauded for its innovative technique. It's the extra arms. They make a difference.

—Could you do me a favor (I hefted him, because he was about to fall) and move a little bit?

—Why?

—Your tentacles are in my face. I can't see very well.

—But I'm comfortable.

—If you don't move, we'll fall down the stairs and become splotches of blood on the ground. This has to be a collaborative effort.

Gregory didn't understand that sometimes, octopuses should go on diets too.

I walked into a wall.

—Ow! he said. Alright, I get it.

He squirmed.

—It's no fun to be back here, I said.

—You don't know anything about octopus anatomy. Just pretend it isn't there, and you won't see it.

—No, I mean, you're slimy.

—I can't help it. It happens.

After Gregory had adjusted himself, I walked down the hallway, bumping into things.

And then I fell down the stairs.

Of course, I dropped Gregory along the way.

—Are you alright? I asked.

—No.

By this point, a crowd had formed around us. They mumbled excitedly. Somewhere in there, I heard a cry of

—We've got ourselves a wounded octopus!

and a moment later

—Somebody call a doctor!

The crowd parted, and an ambulance drove up. Two people carrying a stretcher came out of the ambulance. They wore all red, even over their eyes.

Nearby, a girl was crying. She petted Gregory on the head as she cried.

—You know, he said, if you give me a kiss, I'll become a human prince.

—Really? she asked.

...It didn't work.

::::::::::::::::::::::::

When Gregory was gone, the crowd left with him.

Nearby was an archway that led into a room with a high ceiling. It was full of big, cushioned chairs, some so large you had to climb to get up them.

—E, I said, is that you?

She turned, looked down, and it was.

—Hey, I said, what are you doing?

—Reading a book, she said. I'm not sure where this castle came from though. Probably we're still somewhere in the neighborhood.

—How's it going?

—Not well. I was sleeping.

—Should I let you get back to that?

—Yeah, I was having a good dream. You were in it.

—What were we doing?

—I don't remember. But I guarantee we weren't flying an airplane, climbing a mountain, or baking cupcakes.

—That's good. Cupcakes can be lame, sometimes.

Instead of climbing down, I jumped onto another of the chairs. On the chair beyond that, a girl was playing the violin. Her hands moved but her eyes were closed. A thin scarf hung around her neck. Her hat had something European about it. I've never been to Europe.

—Hello, she said. Do I know you?

—I think we live on the same street. Probably.

—I saw you one day, with your flamethrower. You looked tired.

—That was an unpleasant time in my life. I'm trying to forget it.

—Oh. I understand.

I almost slid down from the chair by accident. I wanted to talk to her some more, but her eyes were closed again. I don't think she could hear me over the music.

I went back to E, and asked if she knew how I could get out of here.

—Sure, she said. There's a hall there that leads out, but be careful.

—Why?

—It's dangerous.

—What do you mean?

—I don't know. It just is, maybe.

That had to be good enough, I guess.

::::::::::::::::::::::

Along the way, I passed a man in a cage—the one who had tackled me a few days ago on the hill. Someday, he whispered, he would destroy me.

::::::::::::::::::::::

I opened a door at the end of the hall. It felt nice to see the sky. Outside, there was a parking lot that went on for miles.

In the parking lot, by the only car, I met a little kid bouncing a ball. Snot leaked down his nose, over his mouth, onto his chin. The red ball he clutched—an icon, like something from an old movie. He made me sad for some reason. Probably because he was crying.

The car next to him was red too. Beside it, a woman with her dark hair tied back.

Her boots were really tall, with pointy heels.

—I have something to tell you, she said.

I nodded.

—Look over there (meaning the horizon, I was pretty sure). Do you see my husband?

—Umm.

—*He's so far away!* she cried. *Beyond reach, passing out of memory!*

—Is that him? I asked.

A few miles away, someone was flying one of those old style planes. It had spinning propellers on the front, with an open cockpit—except it was tied to the ground by a really long string. A big banner trailed from the back of the plane. It read "SOS" in attention catching letters.

—*He's left me,* she wailed, *for the sky, to go on a great journey!*

—I'm sorry.

—Don't worry. (She fixed her posture, straightened her hair.) I'm fine.

—Oh, I said. That's good.

—Would you like to get in the car? There's enough room in there for two.

—Isn't that your son, right there?

—No, she said. I'm not really sure what he's doing here.

—Okay.

She got close, dragged me by the wrist, opened the door, and threw me in so hard I hit my head on the other side. Then she punched me in the face, and apologized; then did it again.

She was all boob.

When she kissed me I thought she was going to swallow my face. Her fingernails made my neck bleed. Whenever I moved, she would put her hands on my shoulders and push me back into the chair.

It was still pretty nice, except whenever I tried to get up again she would punch me in the face. That sort of ruined it for me, a little.

—Sorry about the bruises, she said, when it was done. I'm just very passionate.

—Yeah, I said. I noticed. It's fine.

—Do I know you? I feel like I know you from somewhere.

—Probably not. I don't even think I know myself.

—Really, are you all right?

—It's no problem. Don't worry about it.

I got out of the car twenty minutes later, feeling exhausted, and walked towards the edge of the asphalt. The sun was setting darker now, so even the sky was stained dark red, and the neighborhood below it.

48

I brought one hand to my mouth and looked at it. Blood.

We matched.

GREEN

The neighborhood turned green again.

I stood with M in the sunlight.

M's problems were getting worse. Rings of darkness hung around his eyes. His hair was frayed, broken at the ends, charred and ashy. The color of his skin matched his bones. His body bent. Part of him (the invisible part) was no longer attached to this universe.

"I've seen things," he said, "that you wouldn't believe."

"You would be surprised," I replied.

He told me a story.

::::::::::::::::::::::

I listened.

::::::::::::::::::::::

Whenever I remember what he said, I put it in my own words. Which isn't surprising, because that's how I remember everything else. (I certainly can't remember any other way.)

A long time ago, M was walking in the desert. For every step, he took exactly one breath. Each breath reminded him of his thirst.

And he walked very far.

"I was walking in the desert," he said. "And then I came to a pool." Except the pool was so large it might have been a lake, and it was at the base of a pyramid.

"I had to drink the water," he said, "except instead of just drinking it, I jumped in. It felt nice. Like I'd died and the water was bringing me back to life. Like it was knitting me back together."

For a long time, he just floated on the surface of the water. The desert wasn't so bad, he decided, when you were floating.

"But then I looked back," he said, "and saw that part of me was still standing on the edge. I'd lost something. And I realized that I wasn't the one in the water.

"I was the one looking down."

::::::::::::::::::::::

There had always been something sad about M. There had always been something missing. Even on such a bright day, I could hardly even see him.

"What do you think?" he asked.

"That was a fascinating story," I said. "There's only one problem."

"What's that?"

"Look around," I said. "There's no desert for miles."

::::::::::::::::::::::

"Look," he said, "do you see it?" He walked with his head down, muttering sometimes under his breath. His clothes hadn't been washed for days. His limbs dragged like the strings of a puppet, but with no puppeteer.

"What?"

"In the sky, there's an eye watching us."

"I don't see anything," I said.

"It's there," he said. "There's an eye."

I blinked.

::::::::::::::::::::::

"Are you alright?" I asked. "You're bleeding."

M clasped his arm, from which blood spilled profusely. In streaks, in trails, more ran along his back, his neck, coating the shirt he wore. Capillaries burst in his eyes; a gout spurted from his temple. Black light shone in and out of his face. His heart throbbed so strongly it vibrated the air.

"No," he said, "my body doesn't work anymore."

"What happened?" Though in truth, I already

55

knew.

So much of him, wounded. He gestured to himself: scrapes, gashes, punctured lungs, beheadings, dismemberment, cancerous entities, poison, a protruding blade. Ivory bones, the crushed figure beneath his skin. "This used to be my body," he said. "I went into the world, or the world went into me, and now it doesn't work anymore."

On the last word, he coughed, jarring his insides.

Another followed, and another.

By a stop sign, he vomited a pool of blood so large I wondered how it could all come from one body: seeping, and spreading, an isolated shade against the green, the white, the blue; a spewing geyser casting up a fine spray, like mist, to fleck the surroundings. I'd never seen blood like that. Real blood was darker, it had a function other than to be seen. This was more like a movie: image and symbol. Vehement gouts, but no wound. M's shoulders shook.

Finally, with stains all over his face, and both his feet in the pool, M gasped. I wondered: was there anything left in him, any remnants?

He clasped his stomach and nearly fell.

"Are you alright?"

"Yeah," he said, "just give me a minute."

"I understand. Take as long as you need."

I helped him walk until some of his strength came

back. He left a hardening trail on the ground. Coated in his own blood. Dragging his feet. Barely able to move.

::::::::::::::::::::::

M stumbled. We walked down the road. On either side of us, trees grew in straight lines, making way for the thin strip of the sky, a vague piece of itself. The road had no end or beginning. It led only to itself, and other parts of the neighborhood.

"Look," he said, "do you see that?"

"I think so."

There was a tree in the center of the road: thin, all the leaves swaying without any wind. Its roots sank downward. Into the cement.

"That isn't supposed to be there," I said.

"I figured."

"It looks pretty cool though. Especially for a tree."

M poked the trunk. Something began to move.

"Get back," I said.

I grabbed his shoulder just in time. The leaves shook, and caught fire: a burning rainbow, suspended in the branches.

M was the kind of person who lit trees on fire just by touching them.

::::::::::::::::::::::::

M can't walk places in the dark because whenever he tries, he knocks into things. Piles of things fall on him. Even if he holds out his hands, like a blind person, he still knocks into things.

One time, when I was walking in the darkness, I stumbled over something, and it was him, sprawled on the ground, unable to move. He didn't have eyes anymore. Maggots crawled amidst the remnants of his skin, fibrous muscles like rotted spaghetti. Worms fucked his intestines. Beetles were chewing his brains.

He lifted an arm, displaying skeletal fingers.

"I can't live here anymore," he said "I can't live."

"I know," I said. "There's no help for us in this world. No help for us anywhere."

E jumped out of a tree and I caught her. It was weird but still pretty nice.

"Why do you keep doing that?" I asked.

"When I'm in a tree," she said, "I can see things better. Like in a watchtower."

"Oh."

"It helps me study things."

"Like what?"

"People. For example, you."

"What have you learned?"

"You look at the ground because you don't care where you're going. Sometimes when you're alone you mutter under your breath, like M. Unless certain people are around, you don't smile enough."

She knew everything about me.

M was sitting in a chair with a table by it, playing solitaire. Every few seconds he would scratch his forehead. He frowned.

"What's going on?" I asked.

He looked up. "I've never been very good at this game."

"Yeah," I said, "neither have I."

::::::::::::::::::::::::

I heard a song to one side of the street. It was like a picture, but moving.

A girl sat outside her house, playing the violin. For every sound, her hand moved; but that motion itself was not music, even if it caused the music. She was pretty in the way that girls are pretty.

"I didn't expect to see you again," she said.

"It seems like we meet all the time," I replied, "but never know each other. Isn't that strange?"

It sounds melodramatic, but the only thing stranger than life is everything in it.

She asked if I wanted lemonade. She didn't have lemonade anyway, she only had water; but it didn't matter, I wasn't thirsty.

"So you like music?" I asked.

She shook her head. "I only like playing it. When I hear someone else, it makes me want to hurt things."

"Any idea why?"

She took a drink of water.

"Do you want to go somewhere?"

E shook her head. "I'm happy right here."

We were lying in a bed, parked in a parking lot, outside either a school or a church, I wasn't sure which. Green light wound through the air. We were surrounded by cars, but no one passed on the road. There was nowhere to go.

She tickled me. I kissed her on the nose.

"I love you the way a cup loves water," she said.

"Aww," I said. "I'm touched."

::::::::::::::::::::::

On the other side of the fence, M was working on something. He had a box with metal things in it, and a bunch of other stuff in front of him. Some of it sparkled. The rest was dull, and it didn't sparkle.

When people have rigid brows, you can tell they're concentrating.

"What are you doing?" I asked.

"Building a machine."

"What's it going to do?"

"I'm not sure," he said. "Stuff."

"Something?"

"Yeah." He nodded. "Something."

:::::::::::::::::::::::

I feel like I've been here before.

:::::::::::::::::::::::

The girl sat in her chair. We talked, like two people.

:::::::::::::::::::::::

M was still building his machine. It grew. Pieces of it fit together like the inside of a computer. He used a wrench to put the pieces together. He wiped his face with a white cloth. He ate potato chips and a sandwich.

:::::::::::::::::::::::

A hand came out of the ground and grabbed onto my foot. I tried to shake it off, but it wouldn't let go, because it had fingers. I tried to go somewhere else, but I couldn't, because there was a hand holding onto my ankle. I closed my eyes, but it was still there. Even if I couldn't see it.

"Hello," said E. "I got you."

"You were hiding?" I asked. "Again?"

"Aren't I stealthy?"

"I thought you were something scary. Like a monster."

"I'm offended."

"I can't help it. I was scared."

"Oh."

It wasn't a fight exactly, but it was a little awkward.

::::::::::::::::::::::

Along the road, almost by accident, I saw a bunch of people with the heads of animals, grazing. They held teacups in their hands, over saucers, conversing in small groups of two to six, with good posture. One wore a button up shirt: horse-face. Another had on a tuxedo: oxen. A third, khaki shorts and a tank top: buzzard. Their faces protruded, pressing outward. Their bodies seemed to be on stilts because of how tall they were. Many, donning respectable watches, probably had work soon, or had recently come from the office. They reminded me of things I don't think about. Most of the time.

::::::::::::::::::::::

We spent the day in E's house watching movies, except at some point both of us fell asleep. We were on a couch in a room with a big window that spanned an entire wall.

"Are you all right?" I asked.

E opened her eyes. Just barely. "I think, maybe." Out the window, fish swam in a pond. Her lips: a color. They opened and closed. The TV made no sound; she didn't want to fall into it. It's not safe to jump into televisions.

"Come here," she said. "I want to tell you something." I put my ear by her mouth. She whispered. She pulled me closer. She pressed her lips against my eye.

Her eyes closed. That was all I saw. A little light and some greater closeness.

"Give me a kiss," she said. "I want to see what you taste like."

"A person, probably."

"That's possible," she said. "I just need to be sure."

DARK GREEN

Along one side of the street, the old man was attempting to hide beneath a bush. He wasn't any good. His shoulders stuck out, his teeth chattered, his eyes glowed. The light hit him all wrong, like a buried skull, the kind scavengers chew. He resembled a snake, curling in the branches, but without any camouflage. He hissed.

His wrists were extremely thin.

::::::::::::::::::::::

M was still working on his machine, except now, he was much closer to done. It was big, and had a bunch of screens all over it—pressure gauges, leaking fluid, humps like an insect, blinking lights.

"It's impressive," I said. "Do you know what it does yet?"

"It's either a time machine or a door to another dimension. I'm still not sure."

"Are you sure that's all? There has to be something else."

"Like what?"

There's always something else.

::::::::::::::::::::

The old man hid between buildings in an alley, holding his cane. He was getting cleverer now. He was planning ambushes.

He crept closer. He had a big grin on his face, turning the teeth downward: a crescent moon facing the wrong way. His suit helped him blend in with the darkness. He held the cane above his head, poised to strike, except there wasn't anyone there, and no one was coming, either.

Whenever his knees bent, the joints cracked.

::::::::::::::::::::

M stood up. He had dirt on his face, and I don't think he'd eaten for hours. His eyes told me he was thinking of someplace far away where the neighborhood was better, at least for him. Someday, I hoped he'd be able to go there, at least for a little while.

::::::::::::::::::::

The old man was very bald. The first thing you noticed about him was baldness, and wisps of white around the baldness, like orbiting moons, to accentuate how bald he was, the splotchiness of the skin there. If you looked at him he would try to kill you. He didn't take well to being seen.

"What is your earliest memory?" I asked.

"Being born."

"Really?"

"When I came out of my mother, the first thing the doctors noticed was that I had teeth. I bit into one of their hands and chewed on it. The nurse screamed, but when she went into another room I chased after her, and started eating her legs. One of the orderlies stepped on my head by accident. I've never gotten over that.

"Finally, once everything had calmed down, they handed me back to my mother. For a couple of minutes, I cried. She hugged me really close. I remember that her skin was damp, and she smelled funny because she'd just gotten done giving birth.

"After that, I bit off her left breast." He shook his head. "Nothing's been right between us ever since."

"Oh," I said. "You haven't changed very much."

M accidentally dropped something heavy on his thumb.

"Ow," he said.

"You okay?" I asked.

He put the damaged finger in his mouth, to lick away the blood.

"Yeah," he said, "I'm fine."

::::::::::::::::::::::

The old man wore a wreath of leaves on his head, as though he were attempting to hide in the jungle, or sacrifice babies to some sybaritic god. On each cheek, he'd streaked great bands of color to mark the cavernous surface. His eyes were yellow already, so he didn't have to touch them. He gnashed his teeth.

"What are you doing?" I asked.

"I'm hunting children."

"Oh. I figured. Is it going well?"

He shook his head. "All I've seen today is middle-aged women going to church."

"It's Sunday," I said. "I guess I'm not surprised."

"One had a little girl with her." He growled, clenching his fist. "I tried to take the little girl, except her mother hit me with her purse. I think the purse had rocks in it. My face hurts." His eyes turned somewhere far away. The snake, curling on its pole, licked itself and hissed.

"What do you do when you aren't here?" I asked.

"I listen to old radio programs," he said, "and tenderize raw meat. Sometimes I like checkers, but no one is willing to play with me."

"Is that it?"

"I collect stamps, postcards, and books on the apocalypse." He coughed. "Stop asking me questions."

I bit my bottom lip.

:::::::::::::::::::::::

M knelt in the midst of his machine. Fingers of blue lightning surrounded him. He put something in place and fastened it there with his wrench. Then he moved on to something else.

:::::::::::::::::::::::

The old man was trying to climb a telephone pole with the wrong gear. He had snowshoes, a pickax, two hundred feet of rope, and a parachute. He was back to lurking on street-corners.

"What are you trying to do?" I asked.

"Getting leverage. I'll swoop like a hawk."

"That's very creative."

"I thought so." He wiped some of the sweat from his forehead. "Beware. I am on the hunt."

"Are you sure you want to go up there?"

On the top of the pole already, in front the electric

lines, was perched a gigantic eagle (at least, it looked like an eagle), wielding a curved beak, its wings extended twenty feet in either direction, raining broad feathers. Its eyes raped the distance. I wouldn't have gone near it with anything short of a light saber.

The old man chuckled.

"That?" he said. "It's nothing. I could take it down with my bare hands."

"Alright. If you say so."

"I'm not afraid of anything." He was trying to sound like a soldier. "Not lions, bears, or tigers. Not anything, you hear me?" Both his eyes trained deeply into the past. "I'm not afraid. Of anything."

I wonder who he was talking to.

::::::::::::::::::::::

I got the feeling something bad was going to happen.

::::::::::::::::::::::

Something bad happened.

M came to me to me as I was sitting someplace, thinking. Sometimes I think too much.

Just maybe.

"What's going on?" I asked.

"E's missing," said M. He was looking worried.

Worry shot out of his face and worry was a part of his mouth. Worry was in his breath and his eyes. Worry was the driving force behind his body. "I've looked everywhere but I can't find her." He clasped his stomach, because he'd been running. "I'm worried."

"So am I."

"Do you know where she would be?"

"I might have an idea."

I said, "Follow me."

Dark colors fell around the world, just a little, even if I couldn't see them.

::::::::::::::::::::::

I searched in the trees, in bushes, and even under the ground, but no matter how hard I looked I couldn't find her. In the past, pretty often, we'd been in separate places, both of us—but up until now I'd never been worried that she didn't exist anymore.

It felt different, somehow.

::::::::::::::::::::::

After that, I got a feeling.

::::::::::::::::::::::

The old man lived on that corner where he always stood. Unsurprisingly, his house was very old, like he was, though he was even older.

Its walls were yellow the way parchment is yellow, like the light from old lamps in musty parlors, decorating ashtrays, beneath quiet paintings, to soft music in the next room, coming from instruments nobody played anymore, turned rusty inside, so that nothing came out when you blew them, except the past.

The door let us in. We went inside. There wasn't anything interesting to see, so I didn't look at anything.

We went down the hallways. We went through the kitchen, opening another door. We passed by the bathroom. We saw the skeleton of the old man's dog. He'd once owned a parakeet, and that was dead too, a perched sculpture of bones standing in its cage.

We found E tied to a sort of makeshift altar. She was sleeping in such a way that I'm sure it hurt her neck, moving softly as she slept, because she was still breathing.

"Hey," I said.

She opened her eyes until they saw me. They were the same color I remembered them being. They were still eyes.

"Hey," she said. "I'm glad you're here. He was going to sacrifice me. I didn't really feel like being sacrificed."

"That makes sense," I said. "I wouldn't want to be sacrificed either."

We untied her and she said she was hungry. The old man didn't have any food in his house. He believed in eating everything raw.

The floor creaked as we walked on it.

Just as we were about to leave, the door opened, and the old man saw us. His eyes got all big, and he lunged. He was thinking about finality. I'd always been too fast for him, but that was in the past, and in the present nothing worked the same, everything was different.

I picked up an ashtray and threw it. It hit him in the face, and he died. Afterwards, he just laid there. Not moving. I poked him a few times with a fork M handed me, and he was still dead. I hit him with a pillow, and he didn't come back to life.

Until the end of the world, he would have bits of squirrel stuck between his teeth.

::::::::::::::::::::::

Before we left, I picked up his cane. It hissed at me, and it was kind of cute. Obviously, I wasn't willing to pet it—but in case someone wanted to see, I stuck the bottom in the yard and built a cage around it. I put up a sign that said:

"Beware of Fangs."

I wondered if anyone would listen.

:::::::::::::::::::::::

"Are you all right?" I asked.

"I'm doing okay," E said.

"How was it?"

"Icky. I didn't like his house very much."

"He's been going tribal recently. I should have known."

"Yeah," she said. "He was going to sacrifice me to the god of roast pork."

"Roast pork?"

"The other day he killed a guinea pig and ate it. I think that's why."

"I don't get it."

"No," she said. "Neither do I."

M and I stood for a while, just looking at his machine. I was afraid it was going to eat me.

"I'm curious," I said. "What made you want to build this thing?" When I have a surplus of creative energy, I throw rocks into the river and think about where they'll be in a few million years. (I haven't figured it out yet, so I'm still interested.)

M put his hands in his pockets.

"I don't know." He shrugged. "It's something to do, I guess."

::::::::::::::::::::::::

The machine was alive.

::::::::::::::::::::::::

We heard something like an explosion, of electricity. Imagine that the sky was made of glass—and then it broke. The ground began to move. Thick liquid started to leak out of the hole in the sun.

It felt like the entire world slanted, to a point where

distances met.

But then it slanted so much both of us fell off, and I realized that yeah, it had eaten us after all.

:::::::::::::::::::::::

M and I were on an island. The sky was purple, and the trees looked like flowers. It would have been pretty cool if I hadn't felt so nauseous from the fall.

"Hello," said a voice. It belonged to a creature made of purple lines and balloons, each attached in place of joints. Its whole body swayed, drifting upwards without permission. "Are you looking for the mountain?"

M nodded. "We are."

Our eyes followed the direction it pointed. "Go that way," it said. "When you come to the edge of the platform, you should reach the mountain eventually, if you really want to go there."

M nodded again. "We do."

"Be careful," said the body made of balloons.

M mouthed, "We will," but no sound came out. His eyes were impossibly dilated, entirely without focus.

I wonder what he was thinking about.

:::::::::::::::::::::::

The mountain was the biggest object in all of existence. It poked through the top and bottom of the universe. Everything else orbited it, because it was so big. It was made of uncreation, of nothingness.

There was no valley.

I said something, but M didn't respond. All the color had gone from his eyes, staring nowhere, contemplating sparks.

He was quiet for nearly five minutes, but just when I thought he'd forgotten I was there, he said:

"I need to see."

See what?

"Down there," he said. "Beneath the mountain."

"Are you sure?" I asked. "There's nothing there. Nothing at all."

He shook his head. "I've never been more certain of anything in my life." He raised his arms. "Look up. Can you see?"

I could.

Directly above us there was an eye, like the one M had seen on the street. I could only see the outline of it, but it was there, with no clouds to hide it now. The only places it couldn't see didn't exist, but M wanted to go there too.

I never replied.

M walked to the edge and jumped—or he dove, holding both hands in front of his face, like a drop of rain with a human body. He fell, and fell, and fell, in silence, because falling doesn't make a sound; until finally he turned invisible too, because he was too far away, and I couldn't see him anymore.

:::::::::::::::::::::::

Either side of the hallway was lit with lamps, but it was still dark. I'd been walking for a long time. The only person I passed was a little man carrying an empty glass on a tray. Pretentious, he pretended he knew where he was going, even if I'm sure he didn't.

At the end of the hallway, I opened a door.

In a tall, hard backed chair, her profile facing the fireplace, I saw a girl playing the violin. As always, the girl played with her eyes shut. Everything was European about her, but I don't know how. I've never been to Europe.

:::::::::::::::::::::::

She stopped playing and turned to me.

Her movements were lithe, even when she wasn't moving.

"I didn't think you would find me here," she said. "This is where I go when I want to be alone."

"I'm sorry."

"It's fine. I was just about to leave, but I'm not sure if I plan on coming back. I don't belong here. I realize that now."

"Where will you go?"

"Somewhere."

I laughed. I wonder if she thought I was being rude.

Probably.

"I've said this before," I said, "but you play violin really well. I wish I was that good at something. Anything."

"Thank you." She closed her eyes. "Mostly I just play music when I'm alone."

"Where do I know you from?" suspended in yellow memory. "I've seen you before, but I mean before that."

"I don't know," she said. "I don't remember either."

"What about you?" I asked. "Have you ever been to Europe?"

She shook her head. "Never."

::::::::::::::::::::::

I didn't see M again for a really long time. When he finally came out of the portal, he looked haggard. He hadn't eaten in days. His clothes were dusty. Hollowness scoured his face—I don't know what that means but his face was scoured. Every thought was banished. Every notion of future.

He told me a story.

These are his words this time, because I remember them.

"I fell a really long ways," he said.

"I figured. That's what it looked like."

"Later, I woke up in another field full of flowers. All of them hung above my head, a bunch of different colors but with their petals spreading out. I got up and started to walk. Then, I came to the edge of a town."

"Did you recognize it?"

"No, I don't think so. Anyway there wasn't anyone in it, so it doesn't matter, and I couldn't read the words on any of the signs. A gray mist hung above everything, like a fog. When I got hungry, I took a candy bar from a store. I went to sleep in a car and woke up a few hours later. There was a girl standing in front me."

"Did you recognize her?"

"Yeah," he said. "I've seen you talking to her. She's normally playing a violin. Know who I'm talking about?"

Yeah, I replied, I knew.

"She told me some strange things about you."

My skin shivered. "I don't want to know."

"Not even where you came from? You haven't

always here, she said, in the neighborhood. Which is strange, because I thought everyone came from the neighborhood."

"No," I said. "Not even where I came from."

I remember nothing.

"She told me I was lost," M continued, "and that if I stayed there long enough, I might never go back. And then I realized something."

"What?"

"I couldn't see." He scraped his face. Something was breaking, shapeless upwelling. "That eye in the sky was gone. I'd gotten so used to it I hardly noticed. But it's still gone. And I notice now."

M began to cry. Tears of blood streamed down his face. His fingernails broke open the skin, cleaving gouges—a streaming mask, except he couldn't take it off. He couldn't take it off.

Ever.

"I'm sorry," I said. "Maybe eventually it'll come back."

"It won't," he replied. "That isn't how it works."

"I don't know what to say."

"Do you know what the worst part of it is?" he asked. "I didn't get the rest of myself back. That part of me is still in the desert, swimming; but because of him now my body doesn't work. When I touch my skin I can't feel it. Even if you said something, I'm not sure

I'd be able to hear."

::::::::::::::::::::::::

She turned towards me. She spoke.

"I knew you before," said her eyes, "in a different life."

It must have been difficult to say, even without speaking—but it was nearly impossible to hear.

All the walls, I noticed, were covered in red velvet.

::::::::::::::::::::::::

"Did anything else happen?" I asked.

"Probably," said M. "All I know is that, eventually, I came to bridge. The bridge took me over a dark sea. There were other bridges in the distance, too many to count, except none of them led anywhere. Sometimes they trailed off into the water, or even sank, one end sticking up just barely.

"When I got to the other side," he continued, "I was here."

"That doesn't seem right," I said. "I thought you came out of the portal, but I'm not even sure."

"I know. It's strange."

"Does it mean anything?"

"I'm not sure. Now, I'll never know."

He was looking better now, but still bad. Dry blood in his hair: sticky black clumps. He could hardly stand up straight. His body was shaped like a skeleton, and not just because he had bones beneath his skin. His eyes rolled along the ground, but he didn't have the strength to put them back.

I walked beneath a tree and E jumped out of it. This time she landed on me and knocked me down, but I didn't really mind.

"When you were gone," she said, "I missed you."

"I missed you too."

"Make me a promise."

"Anything."

"Never sacrifice someone to a pagan god. No matter what happens."

"Can I tell you a secret?"

"As long as you don't mind if I know it."

"I wasn't planning on sacrificing anyone anyway."

I kissed her forehead.

She giggled.

::::::::::::::::::::::::

A creature on wings circled the mountain. The mountain went so high it was practically an airplane that didn't fly; so tall it could impale the moon. The tip of it was pointed like a spear. Its sides were dark black all the way up.

:::::::::::::::::::::::

"Do you remember the last time we were here?" I asked. "You gave me a gift."

"Sometimes I'm nice like that," she replied. "Sometimes."

"This is where we climbed the flower," I said. "Look. Except now there's a fire."

We didn't feel like climbing again anyway.

Instead, we found a leaf and tossed it into the fire.

:::::::::::::::::::::::

Sometimes when I looked into the distance, I remembered that the darkness I could see there was actually the mountain, holding up the base of the universe. If I were to walk that way, the neighborhood would never end, but eventually it would become less real—there would be people there, and houses, but the people would be ghosts, and the houses would be empty. Along the way I would pass an immense castle, where a little while ago I'd wanted to kill an octopus. In front of it there would be a road. The road continued even where the world began to change colors. And then, just for a second, a green light would flicker on the horizon. Usually green is reserved for the trees. Usually

88

green is just a part of life—but then it would be different, somehow. In the sky would be a hole, and beneath the hole would be the mountain. Dimensions crossed here and planes of thought crossed here. Below the mountain was a black pit, and that pit was nothingness. Except, at the same time, it was everywhere, within us and outside us. Above the darkness was a field of color, and we were in that field—the field goes on infinitely, as all things continue inside it. When you come close enough to the mountain, the ground breaks away; and all you can see are a mass of red vessels in the sky, with sails. The red vessels can take you to other parts of the mountain. Mostly they would be empty, but some weren't—they had people and things in them, and they came. A long time ago, I'd been in one. Where I'd come from. I wondered if the girl with the violin had come with me. Sometimes I wonder about a lot of things.

::::::::::::::::::::::

The world was changing color again.

BLUE

I can't see into anyone else's room. All day, I sit on my bed, maybe looking at the walls, both hands folded over my lap. Sometimes I hear sounds, but I never know where they're coming from. When it's absolutely necessary I drink a glass of water.

I block out the light, every surface. As I move, my shadow moves: a duplicate, sheared from blue. At night, I go to sleep, but I can't tell when it's morning. Everything is night, even (especially) the day.

Sometimes when it's cold enough, I get beneath the covers, or hide under my bed. No one can find me there. Anyway, I don't know anyone who would care to look.

::::::::::::::::::::::

Blue light covers the street when I look out my window. Blue light hangs heavy in the curtains when I part them. The sidewalk sits on top of the street like a carpet, but no one walks on it. I hardly ever see people, but only empty places where they aren't.

Either way, the light stays the same. My room contains a table, a bed, a window, and me. Every day I talk to myself, but I don't listen very well. Everything is quiet.

The moon has returned from the sky.

::::::::::::::::::::::

You came back, I said. The words were in my mouth, but I let go of them. That's all that happens, when I speak.

I missed this place. I missed this neighborhood.

The cold is back. I can see the ghosts again.

Sometime we say such strange things, eradicating ourselves.

I think this was one of those times.

::::::::::::::::::::::

Along the street, I passed a fence made of spears, each about eight feet tall. Anyone who tried to climb them would probably get impaled. On top already were a few people that hadn't been cleaned off—for some reason, they hadn't noticed the open gate nearby.

Through the barrier, a horse was looking at me. Green streaks stirred around its eyes; sharp teeth lacerated the corners of its mouth. Blood dripped along its muzzle, pointed like a beak, except with teeth, and nostrils above it. It was chewing something, I couldn't tell what.

A radish.

::::::::::::::::::::::

I met Mr. B in the park. He was reading the sky, even if there were hardly any words in it today.

When the sky moves, he said, *you can tell something is going to happen.*

You're right, I said. *Something is.*

He raised a hand.

The bush rustled. Something looked out at us, with two eyes.

You see that bridge there? He pointed.

Really the mist covered most of it, but I nodded. Certain parts went over the river, hanging in air. It held up cars and the sky. The clouds hardly paid attention to it.

Mr. B took a drink of coffee.

::::::::::::::::::::::

Beneath a streetlight, someone was waiting for me. He folded both arms in front of his chest, chin tilted, wearing a jacket even if it wasn't cold. It was the guy who hated me, who had tackled me in the snow.

You're back, I said. *Have I done something else?*

You murdered me!

If anything, I blame the bear.

No. He shook his head. *You shouldn't have left me in that cage*

I don't know, I said. *I figured there was a good reason you were there.*

He frustrated me.

How did you come here? I asked. *M's machine, right?*

Dimmed by contradictory yellow; the mist behind. He pulled a big stick from his back, and waved it like a torch—but no fire, no fire anywhere. Nothing could burn in air this damp.

I'll have my revenge, he said.

Look out, I said. *There's an eel behind you.*

You won't fool me, he replied. *I won't turn around.*

I'd lied, of course—really the eel looked more like a snake, hovering in air, wrenching its jaws. Its long body curled, blending with vapor; eyes so narrow it must have been difficult to see. It carried an aura of fire too, but impossible to make out, blended into things. Drifting, it hardly made a sound, subtly caped, no slither.

He was carried away by foxes.

::::::::::::::::::::::

The water rose.

Little pools slid between cracks in the sidewalk, splashing wherever I walked, making dry socks impossible. The sea invaded the land—then the rains came, doubling the water. One river rose up and flowed between all the buildings. Occasionally, it was possible to spot a fish, but not often.

I asked Mr. B if he knew how to swim. He said he did, but he'd never been a lifeguard.

Community pools are dangerous, I said. *They're only good for drowning small children. That's why the only people who go there are mothers.*

Mr. B nodded. I think he really felt things sometimes, even if they were too ugly. *Nobody watches this world, he said. It's our fault, for having only two pairs of eyes.*

Is that what's wrong, you think?

The water rose.

Sometimes, I said, *I wonder about things.*

Mr. B nodded. *That happens.*

Eventually, everything would be dark.

Eventually, everywhere would be the bottom of the sea.

::::::::::::::::::::::

I went back to my room because there wasn't anywhere else to go.

Water sloshed against the building. I shut the window, to keep myself from hearing it.

In the corner of the room, hands folded around her knees, white light shining from her, The Moon was waiting for something.

The tides are rising, I said. *The world is becoming water. Is it my fault?*

I set my head against the wall.

Remember: E doesn't mind. She's the one who invited you.

The Moon laughed. *She doesn't mind sharing because there's only one of us—her and me, in her body. Isn't she the best?*

She was.

Waves crashed against the window; and for a second, it felt like we were on the outside again, except now everything was becoming ocean. If the wave had its way, it would bash our heads against rocks, and we would die.

Look at the tides.

BLACK

The whole neighborhood drowned, and everything was dark.

I clung to the same piece of driftwood for like two weeks, and it really sucked.

GREEN

E was looking at a flower. Then she held it up to the sun for a second, until it caught on fire.

"Hey," she said. "When I saw you words came into my head, I'm not sure which ones though."

"Goods words?"

"I don't know. Probably."

She stepped back.

"Let's go somewhere," she said.

"Where?"

"A place."

We went.

To the forest. Then we stood at the top of a hill for a while.

"From here," I said, "you can see really far. Through things."

She nodded.

:::::::::::::::::::::::

Did I say anything about color?

::::::::::::::::::::::

M curled beneath a table. He reached both hands around his knees. He laid his head against them. Even in his dreams, he heard my eyes.

"Sorry," he said. "I think I was asleep."

"Did something happen?" I asked.

"I got tired."

"Oh," I replied. "That makes sense." I pulled a chair away to make room. "Why a table?"

"Sometimes I just like to be under tables," he said. "It makes me feel secure."

He squeezed from where he was sitting. For the most part he was looking better. Some color had come back to his skin, and he had pupils again. That's all that mattered, really.

"Have you been doing anything interesting lately?" I asked.

"Not really," he said. "Mostly I just sleep."

"What about your dreams?"

"They aren't so bad, most of the time."

"Do you think you'll be all right?"

He paused, and sighed, and looked down, but there was hardly any emptiness in him. Maybe he even saw. That would be good. That would definitely be a good thing.

"Yeah," he said. "I'll be all right."

::::::::::::::::::::

E and I walked beneath a waterfall. Then we sat for a while, and dried. Then we walked beneath the waterfall again, and it was all very impractical.

::::::::::::::::::::

"Are you sure?" I asked. "You're feeling better?"

M hung his head. Maybe someday the rest of him would come back, too.

"Don't worry," he said.

::::::::::::::::::::

I want to talk about color, but there's nothing left to say.

CPSIA information can be obtained at www.ICGtesting.com
Printed in the USA
BVOW08s1957300715

410899BV00002B/3/P